HELP!
I'M TRAPPED IN
A SUPERMODEL'S BODY

HELP!
I'M TRAPPED IN
A SUPERMODEL'S BODY

TODD STRASSER

AN
APPLE
PAPERBACK

SCHOLASTIC INC.
New York Toronto London Auckland Sydney
Mexico City New Delhi Hong Kong

ISBN 0-439-21035-6

12 11 10 9 8 7 6 5 4 3 2 1   1 2 3 4 5/0

Printed in the U.S.A.   40

First Scholastic printing, February 2001

To Catherine Charles Schrage,
inventor of the Goof Pot

HELP!
I'M TRAPPED IN
A SUPERMODEL'S BODY

1

In my kitchen, Amber Sweeny, the smartest person and prettiest girl in our grade, swept her blond hair out of her face, leaned back in her chair, and blew a perfect saliva bubble.

"How do you do it?" I asked.

Amber flashed a brilliant smile. "I don't know. I just do."

"How come mine keep popping on the tip of my tongue?" my friend Andy Kent asked.

"Your saliva's not wet enough," Amber replied.

"How can saliva not be wet enough?" asked my friend Josh Hopka.

"All I know is that if it's too wet, you can't make the bubbles," Amber explained. "And if it's not wet enough, you can make them but they pop on the tip of your tongue."

She rolled her tongue and another perfectly clear saliva bubble formed on the tip. She gave a little puff and the bubble took off and floated down to the table where it popped.

"Show-off," Josh grumbled.

"Hey, check this out." I pointed at a photo of a sleek red sports car in the magazine I was reading. "The Ferrari Superrossa."

"Who cares?" Andy said. "It's just a car."

"It's not *just* a car," I corrected him. "It's the fastest and most expensive car in the world."

"It would be so cool if you had one," Amber said dreamily.

"What's the point?" Josh asked. "It would just sit in the driveway. You can't drive."

"Jessica could drive it for him," Andy said. "She just got her license, didn't she?"

"Yup." I nodded.

"Jessica can drive?" Amber asked in awe. Jessica may have been my older sister, but to us she was still a kid.

"She'll do *anything* to use the car," I said. "Yesterday she took Lance to the veterinarian, picked up the dry cleaning, and even went grocery shopping."

"That's so cool," Andy said. "We'll have our own taxi service."

At that exact moment Jessica came into the kitchen. She had the mail in her hands. "Exactly not!"

"But you'll get to use the car," Josh said.

"Forget it," Jessica replied as she sorted through the letters. "There's no way I'm going to be Jake's personal chauffeur."

2

My sister tossed me a bright pink envelope. "This one's for you, Jake."

The return address said *Supermodel Today* magazine.

"Get real." I tried to hand it back. "It has to be yours."

"From *Supermodel Today*?" Jessica shook her head. "Not a chance. I wouldn't be caught dead."

I dropped the unopened letter to the table. "Neither would I."

Amber picked up the envelope. "If no one else is going to open it, I guess I will."

She pulled out a pale pink letter and started to read: "Congratulations, Jake Sherman, you have won *Supermodel Today* magazine's 'Personal Assistant to a Supermodel Contest.'"

Jessica clasped her hands. "Way to go, Jake!"

"It's a joke," I said.

"Looks real to me." Amber handed me the letter. It smelled like perfume. "It's not a form letter or anything. Someone named Fiona Charm signed it."

Amber was right. The letter appeared to be directed only to me. Fiona Charm was the beauty editor.

"This is weird," I said. "It says that I'll be able to work with the supermodel right here in Jeffersonville. I don't get it. How did this happen?"

I heard what sounded like snickers and looked up from the letter. Josh's and Andy's faces were red, and they were covering their mouths with their hands as if they were trying really hard not to laugh.

2

"What do you guys know about this?" I asked.

"Us?" Andy answered innocently. "Nothing."

"Give me a break," I muttered.

"I know!" Amber realized. "They must have entered you in the contest!"

"How?" I asked, knowing my friends weren't exactly the types who read *Supermodel Today* magazine.

"At the mall," said Josh.

"There was a poster for the contest in some store," added Andy.

"But we never thought you'd win," concluded Josh, with a big grin.

"Who's the model you're supposed to be the assistant to?" Jessica asked.

I looked back at the pink letter. "Doesn't say."

"What supermodel would want to come to Jeffersonville?" Amber asked. "This is the middle of nowhere."

"Maybe she's so dumb she doesn't know that," Jessica cracked. "After all, they're not exactly known for their brains."

"Whoa!" said Andy. "That's a gross generalization."

Josh wagged a finger at my sister. "You're being very unfair."

"Oh, please." Jessica groaned. "Is it fair that they're all six feet tall and skinny and gorgeous? Is it fair that they get paid millions of dollars just to stand around and smile? Is it fair that they travel all over the world and party with millionaires and movie stars?"

Andy grinned. "Someone sounds seriously jealous."

"Jealous?" Jessica repeated. "No way! Not in a zillion years would I *ever* be a model. I want people to admire me for my brains, not for some superficial thing like beauty."

"Hey, you'll never have to worry about that." I winked.

Jessica made a face. "You're soooo not funny, Jake."

"You really hate models that much?" Josh asked.

"Well, I just think the whole idea is totally twisted, Jessica confirmed.

Josh gave me the slightest smile. Suddenly I knew what he was thinking.

"You know," I said. "Maybe I *will* be a supermodel's assistant after all."

3

Jessica smirked. "You're so full of it, Jake. You're just trying to make me mad. You wouldn't do it in a million years."

"I sure will," I replied.

"Not a prayer." Jessica shook her head and left the kitchen. We heard the front door slam.

"Would you really do it?" Amber asked me after Jessica was gone.

"Get real," I scoffed.

"It would drive your sister totally up the wall," Josh reminded me.

"Listen," I said. "You know I'd do just about *anything* to make my sister crazy."

"Anything *except* be a supermodel's assistant?" Andy guessed.

"You got it," I said.

Amber, Josh, and Andy left a little while later. The next morning, Jessica actually did give me a ride to school. Josh and Andy were going up the walk, and I jogged to catch up to them. We went through the front doors. Without warning, Amanda Gluck planted herself in my path.

"Jake, I want to speak to you in private," she said. Except for Barry Dunn, who is a major bully, Amanda is probably our worst enemy in school. It's not because she wears thick glasses or acts weird and obnoxious. She's just such a brownnosing Goody Two-shoes kiss-up that it drives my friends and me nuts.

"Ooooh! Something's going on." Andy grinned. "Amanda's got a secret."

Snork! Amanda made a strange snorting sound with her nose.

"What was that?" Josh asked.

"Nothing," said Amanda. But then she did it again. *Snork!*

"Doesn't sound like nothing," said Andy. "Sounds like 'snork.' "

"Would you guys just go away and let me talk to Jake?" Amanda said.

The last thing I wanted to do was speak to Amanda in private. "Look, Amanda, whatever you have to say, you can say it in front of my friends."

Amanda came close and whispered in my ear. "It's about a certain cow that's disappeared."

She was talking about the World's Ugliest Cross-eyed Cow, who used to live in a shed behind the school. At one time, for reasons too complicated to explain here, my friends and I had to

9

turn her into the World's Ugliest Cross-eyed Vampire Cow. Now she lived in the woods and only came out at night to drink . . . well, whatever cross-eyed vampire cows like to drink.

"Catch you later, Jakey-poo," Josh teased.

" 'Snork,' Amanda," said Andy.

With big grins on their faces, my friends left.

"So what about the cow?" I asked.

Snork! Amanda made that sound with her nose again.

"What is that?" I asked.

"It's just a stupid nervous habit," Amanda said. "My mom says it'll go away. Now, about the cow, Jake. Sometimes at night she shows up in my backyard."

I can't say I was shocked. Amanda and the World's Ugliest Cross-eyed Cow had once had a special relationship. It wasn't surprising since Amanda couldn't relate at all to people. And as much as my friends and I teased Amanda, I actually felt kind of bad that she'd lost the only true friend she'd ever had.

"Well, Amanda," I said, "I guess she misses you. The good news is that she still likes you enough to visit."

Amanda frowned. "There's something you're not telling me, Jake. And that reminds me of something else. Remember WrestleInsanity?"

I felt a shiver race down my spine. That was

the night Andy, Mr. Dirksen, and I all switched bodies with professional wrestlers.

"I thought you had amnesia," I said.

"I did at first, but now my memory's starting to come back," Amanda said. "I remember you and Andy and Mr. Dirksen weren't in your seats. At the same time, No Nerve Nelson, No Neck Nelson, and The Brainiac were all acting completely strange. Like they'd forgotten how to wrestle."

Amanda gave me a very suspicious look. "I'm really starting to wonder, Jake. It's almost as if you have some way of changing things. Maybe even switching bodies."

I put both hands behind my back and crossed my fingers. "Amanda," I said, "I don't know what you're talking about."

4

The bell rang and it was time to head for home-room. For the next two periods it felt like a typical school day. But then I got to social studies with Ms. Rogers.

Ms. Rogers is this really cute teacher who my friends and I all like. She's married to our science teacher, Mr. Dirksen, who invented the DITS.

"Is it true, Jake?" she asked as soon as the class sat down.

For a moment I didn't know what she was talking about. "Is what true?"

"That you're going to be the personal assistant to Lanny Shanks," Ms. Rogers said.

In a flash, just about every girl in the class turned and stared at me. Murmurs and whispers erupted around the room.

"The supermodel?" Julia Saks realized.

"She was on the cover of *Vogue* last month," added Alex Silver.

"How do *you* know?" Andy asked him.

Alex turned red. "I, er, my mom reads it."

"Isn't she the one who just got that zillion-dollar deal with Poseur Cosmetics?" asked Amber.

"And Angus Bangus of Power Strum is her boyfriend," said Alex. Power Strum was a mad cool band, and Angus was their lead singer.

"Let me guess," said Josh. "You read that in your mom's *Vogue,* too?"

"Actually, it was in *People,*" Alex admitted.

Meanwhile, Julia pulled a copy of *Teen People* magazine out of her backpack. "It says here that Lanny and Angus recently took the Pledge of Veg."

"The what?" asked Andy.

"It's this vegetarian thing all the big stars are doing," Julia reported. "To honor all living things, they won't eat anything that's been killed."

"But plants are living things that have to be killed to be eaten," Andy pointed out.

"Plants don't have brains," said Barry Dunn, the bully.

"Then you must be a plant, Barry," said Josh.

Barry gritted his teeth and made a claw with his hand. It was the sign of the Monkey Bite, a form of torture that Barry specialized in.

Suddenly the PA over the door burst on. "Ms. Rogers?"

"Yes?" our teacher answered.

"Is Jake Sherman in your room?"

"He is," said Ms. Rogers.

"Please send him to Principal Blanco's office immediately."

5

Once again, everyone in the class stared at me. "Uh-oh." Alex Silver grinned. "Maybe you won't get to be Lanny Shanks's personal assistant after all."

"What do you think Blanco wants?" Andy asked.

"The question isn't what Blanco wants," said Julia. "The question is, What did Jake do?"

"I didn't do anything," I sputtered.

"You better go," said Ms. Rogers.

I left the room and started down the hall to the office. I really couldn't figure out what I'd done. Inside the office, Ms. Hub, Principal Blanco's old, white-haired secretary, told me to sit down and wait. A few moments later the door to Principal Blanco's office opened. Principal Blanco is short and pudgy with curly black hair. He gave me a stern look. "Come in, Jake."

He closed the door behind me and then went around to his desk. I sat down. Principal Blanco

15

cupped his hands on his desk and stared silently at me. My heart was pounding. Whatever I'd done, it must have been really serious.

"Jake, how long have we known each other?" he asked.

"Uh, since the beginning of sixth grade," I answered.

"And how often would you say you've been sent down here to see me?"

"Uh, about once every two weeks?" I guessed.

Principal Blanco nodded. "And in all that time, have I always treated you fairly and given you the benefit of every possible doubt?"

"I guess," I replied a little uncertainly. I really couldn't figure out what he was getting at. Principal Blanco gave me a grave and serious look. He'd never acted like this before. My heart started to beat even harder and my chest felt so tight I could hardly breathe.

"Can you trust me to always be fair with you?" he asked.

"I guess," I answered.

Principal Blanco shook his head. "I need more assurance than that, Jake. More than you guess."

"Uh, okay," I said. "Sure, I can trust you to be fair with me. So what's this all about?"

Principal Blanco leaned forward. "If you can trust me, Jake, would it be fair for me to assume that I can trust you?"

"Uh, sure," I said.

"Are you absolutely certain?" Principal Blanco asked.

"Yes."

"Will you give me your word?" My principal held out his hand. "Let's shake on it."

"What are we shaking on?" I asked.

"That I have your word that I can trust you," Principal Blanco replied. "Remember, Jake, a man's word is his, uh . . . I forget, but it's important."

"Er, right," I agreed. This had to be the most bizarre thing ever.

"So we trust each other." Principal Blanco leaned back in his chair and pulled a long gray cardboard tube out from under his desk. He slid it across the blotter to me.

"What's this?" I asked.

"The swimsuit poster."

"Huh?"

"The Lanny Shanks swimsuit poster."

6

I looked at the gray tube and back at my principal. "What am I supposed to do with it?"

Principal Blanco gazed at me as if I was as dumb as a tree stump. "Get it autographed, Jake. And it would be nice if it said something special. You know, not just her signature, but something like . . ." He leaned back in his chair, rubbed his chin, and gazed at the ceiling.

He seemed to be having trouble thinking of something, so I decided to help. "Like something to your daughter?"

Principal Blanco shook his head. "I don't have a daughter."

"Then it's for your wife?" I guessed.

"Heaven forbid!" Principal Blanco placed his hands flat on his desk. "She's not to know *any-thing* about this. Do you understand, Jake?"

I nodded, but the truth was, I didn't understand at all. "Who's it for?"

Principal Blanco gazed steadily back at me.

"You gave me your word, Jake. We shook on it. Do I have your complete trust?"

"Sure, but — "

"No buts, Jake. Do I have your word or not?"

"Er, yes."

"Good." Principal Blanco sat back in his chair and crossed his arms.

"I don't get it," I said.

Principal Blanco raised one eyebrow. "Think about it, Jake."

I still couldn't figure out what he was getting at. "Is it for a niece?"

Principal Blanco let out a big sigh. "It's for *me*, Jake."

It took me a few seconds to understand. Then I had to clench my teeth and press my lips together really hard to keep from smiling.

"We were talking about what Lanny could write on the poster," Principal Blanco reminded me.

"Maybe 'To Principal Blanco — ' "

"No." Principal Blanco shook his head. "Not 'Principal' anything. I want it to be personal."

"I hear you," I said. "How about 'To my favorite school administrator'?"

"No, no, no!" Principal Blanco slapped his hand against the desk. "I've got it! 'To Blancy Wancy, with hugs and kisses.' " He leaned forward on the desk again. "Can you remember that, Jake?"

"It'll be hard to forget, Principal Blanco," I said.

"All right." He nodded. "You may go."

I got up and started to leave.

"Uh, Jake?" Principal Blanco said. "I think you forgot something." He held up the tube with the poster inside.

"Oops! Sorry." I took it and left.

7

Okay, so maybe Principal Blanco had a "thing" for one of the world's most beautiful and famous women. That wasn't so weird, was it?

Well, frankly, yes.

And that wasn't the only weird thing that happened. For the rest of the day, Burp It Up Middle School was gripped with "Lanny fever."

And guess who was at the red-hot center of it all?

At every class change, bunches of giggling sixth- and seventh-grade girls stopped me in the hall to ask if I was really going to meet Lanny Shanks. Guys gave me knowing winks and muttered stuff about how lucky I was. Even the teachers were into it.

"How's it feel to be the most popular kid in school?" Andy asked at lunchtime as he, Josh, and I headed down the hall toward the cafetorium.

"Different," I answered.

"That's for sure." Josh smirked.

A sixth-grader with red hair and glasses came up to us and held out a pad of paper and a pen.

"Jake, can I have your autograph?" he asked.

Andy frowned "What do you want Jake's autograph for?"

"He's famous," said the kid.

I signed my name with a flourish.

"Gee, thanks!" the kid said. "This is so cool! Wait till my friends see!"

My friends and I continued down the hall.

"Would someone please explain to me what makes *you* famous?" Josh asked.

"I guess if you know somebody superfamous, it must make you famous," I said.

"Reality check," Josh said. "You don't *know* Lanny Shanks. You've never even met her. And believe me, she doesn't even know you exist."

"Okay, fine, then I'm just semifamous," I said.

"What does *that* mean?" Andy asked.

"Well, if you're famous when you know someone who's superfamous, then you're semifamous when you don't know them," I said.

"Then *everyone*'s semifamous," Josh argued.

"No," I said. "You can only be semifamous if you're *going* to know someone superfamous."

Josh and Andy glanced at each other.

"Do you want to kill him, or should I?" Josh asked.

"We don't have to." Andy nodded down the hall. "Amanda's going to do it for us."

8

At the end of the hall, just outside the cafetorium doors, Amanda was standing on a chair and taping up a poster that said:

MEDIA STEREOTYPES CAUSE LOW SELF-ESTEEM IN WOMEN

Already up on the wall were posters that said:

THE FACTS ABOUT EATING DISORDERS and THE FACTS ABOUT BODY IMAGE and WHAT APPEARANCE MESSAGES MEAN TO YOU

My friends and I stopped as Amanda climbed down from the chair.

"What's this all about?" Josh asked.

"It's about the warped way that people expect women to look," Amanda replied. "Especially *you*, Jake Sherman."

"Why me?" I asked.

Snork! Amanda made that sound. "Because you've bought into the whole model-as-perfect-woman package."

"I have?" I said.

"You've been brainwashed by . . . *Snork!* . . . the media to believe in unrealistic body types," Amanda announced.

"I have?" I said.

"You entered that . . . *Snork!* . . . contest to be a supermodel's assistant, didn't you?" Amanda asked.

"Not really," I said, then pointed at my friends. "These two bozos entered me."

Josh pointed at Andy. "It was him."

Andy pointed back at Josh. "No, it was *him*."

"You're such a liar," said Josh.

"You're the liar," Andy said. "And you've got an eating disorder. You can't stop eating."

"Well, you've got an *appearance* disorder," Josh shot back. "You can't stop being ugly."

"Oh, yeah? Your *mother* has an appearance disorder," Andy said. "A Halloween pumpkin has more teeth than her."

"Your father has a *brain* disorder," Josh yelled. "He walks you to school because you're in the same grade."

"Your mother has a brain disorder," Andy shouted back. "She's so stupid she sits on the TV and watches the couch!"

"Stop it!" Amanda screamed.

Andy and Josh stopped and stared at her. I'm not sure any of us had ever heard Amanda yell so loudly.

"*Snork!* . . . You've *all* got disorders," Amanda

24

announced. "You all think that . . . *Snork!* . . . women have to be thin and shapely and beautiful."

My friends and I shared puzzled looks. The truth was, except for the occasional MTV babe, I don't think we ever really thought about thin, shapely, or beautiful.

"*You* are the problem," Amanda said.

"Wait a minute," said Josh. "Don't you and your mom have a huge Barbie collection?"

"So?" Amanda said.

"Talk about an unrealistic body type," said Josh.

"But she's . . . *Snork!* . . . a doll," argued Amanda.

"A doll almost every little girl plays with," I said.

"Don't you think little girls wish they could look like Barbie someday?" Josh asked.

"Forget about Bad-Breath Barbie and Belly-Lint Barbie," said Andy. "They ought to have Un-realistic-Body-type Barbie."

"But that would be *every* Barbie," I said.

Amanda's eyes began to well up with tears. "Stop it! This has . . . *Snork!* . . . nothing to do . . . *Snork!* . . . with Barbie! You . . . *Snork!* . . . leave her out of this!"

"You think if Barbie was shaped like Jabba the Hutt she'd be the best-selling doll in history?" Josh asked.

"Forget it," said Andy. "You wouldn't even be able to *give* her away."

"Why . . . *Snork!* . . . do you always . . . *Snork!* . . . have to pick on Barbie?" Amanda wailed.

"We're just trying to show *you* that the reason *you* like Barbie dolls is because they have the exact kind of bodies you say we *shouldn't* like," I said.

"No!" Amanda cried.

"Oh, yeah?" said Andy. "Then where's your Potbelly Barbie?"

"They never . . . *Snork!* . . . made one!" Amanda sobbed.

"How about Cellulite Barbie?" suggested Josh.

"Wide-Bottom Barbie," I said.

"Love-Handle Barbie," said Andy.

"Big-Butt Barbie," said Josh.

Amanda clamped her hands over her ears and screamed, "Stop it! Just . . . *Snork!* . . . stop it!" Then she ran away down the hall.

"Tsk, tsk." Andy shook his head. "The truth hurts."

9

The rest of the day was pure Supermodel Mayhem. I was glad when school was over and there was no one left to ask me to get them Lanny Shanks's autograph or address or phone number. I got home and went into the kitchen for a snack. The kitchen table was covered with magazines like *Glamour* and *Seventeen* and *In Style*.

They were all opened to ads featuring one model. She was tall and thin (no duh! she was a model, for pete's sake!) with thick, shiny blond hair, large, sparkling blue eyes, and the straightest, whitest, most perfect teeth any smile had ever revealed.

I heard the toilet next to the kitchen flush, and then the bathroom door creaked and Jessica came out humming to herself.

"You really ought to wash your hands," I said.

"Drop dead," she growled.

I gestured to the open magazines on the

kitchen table. "I thought you didn't read magazines like these."

Jessica shrugged. "I was just curious."

"About what?" I asked.

My sister frowned at me. "You don't know who that is?"

I shook my head.

"It's Lanny Shanks, you bonehead."

I looked again at the model in the magazines. Lanny Shanks was without a doubt a Major Babe. In fact, she pretty much out-babed all other babes.

"Look at her," Jessica muttered. "See how thin she is? She's a freak. She probably lives on cigarettes, vitamin C, and bottled water. She probably had most of her back teeth pulled out to make her face look thinner. I'll bet she's had a nose job, an eye job, a chin job, a boob job, cheekbones, lips, the works."

"What do they do to your lips?" I asked.

"Inject collagen to make them look fuller," Jessica said.

I winced. "Inject with *needles*? Into her *lips*?"

My sister looked at me like I was an idiot. "What cave have you been living in? This is the twenty-first century. With enough money and operations *anyone* can be beautiful."

"Even Amanda Gluck?" I asked.

Jessica thought for a second. "Okay, *almost* anyone."

28

The phone rang, and my sister answered. "Hello? Yes, this is the Sherman residence. Who? Jake? He's right here. Oh. Really? Hold on."

My sister put her hand over the receiver and held the phone out to me. Her eyes were wide with excitement as she whispered, "It's Lanny Shanks's personal secretary!"

10

I took the phone. "Hello?"

"Jake?" a gruff-sounding woman said. "This is Shiela Shield. Congratulations on winning the contest. Now let's get down to business. Got a piece of paper and a pencil?"

"Sure." I quickly found both. Shiela Shield sounded like the no-nonsense type. The next thing I knew, she was dictating a grocery list to me — lettuce, tomatoes, carrots, avocados, and other stuff.

"I expect to see you and those groceries at Lanny's trailer at the Jeffersonville Mall at five A.M. the day after tomorrow." Shiela sounded really busy and eager to get off the phone.

"Don't you mean five o'clock in the *afternoon?*" I asked. "Five A.M. means five o'clock in the morning."

"I *know* what five A.M. means," Shiela snapped. "If you don't want to be there, I'm sure we can find someone else to be Lanny's personal assistant."

"No, no, I'll be there."

"Good." Shiela Shield hung up.

"What did she want?" Jessica asked as soon as I replaced the receiver on the hook. I told her about the vegetables and having to be at the Jeffersonville Mall at five o'clock in the morning.

My sister frowned. "The mall isn't open at five A.M."

"No, duh," I said.

Jessica went to the refrigerator. "Want something to drink, Jake?"

"Uh, sure," I answered. It was kind of strange for my sister to offer to get me something. Jessica came back to the kitchen table with a couple of Cokes.

"So whatever happened to that miniature version of Mr. Dirksen's body-switching machine?" my sister asked casually.

"You mean, the Mini-DITS?"

"Whatever," Jessica replied.

"It's around somewhere," I said.

"When you say somewhere, you mean, like here in the house?"

I nodded. "Why do you want to know?"

"Oh, no particular reason." Jessica gazed off and didn't say anything more.

11

I was just about to leave for school the next morning when I had the weirdest feeling. It had something to do with the way Jessica had acted the night before. I went up to my room, dug the Mini-DITS out from under the pile of dirty clothes in the back of my closet, and put it in my backpack. Just to be safe, I decided to take it to school.

Later at school, I was taking the Mini-DITS out of my backpack to hide under the pile of dirty clothes in the bottom of my locker when Amanda Gluck shoved a clipboard under my nose.

"Jake, I . . . *Snork!* . . . think you should be the first to sign my — "

Clunk! The Mini-DITS slipped out of my hands and hit the floor.

"You're not . . . *Snork!* . . . supposed to have a portable disc player in school," Ms. Goody Two-shoes said, as I quickly scooped up the Mini-DITS and shoved it into my locker.

"It's not a portable disc player," I blurted.

"Than what . . . *Snork!* . . . is it?" Amanda asked.

Darn! I thought. I'd just made a major mistake. If I'd had half a brain I would have said it was a portable disc player. Now what could I tell her?

"It's nothing."

"Nothing?" Amanda repeated.

"Just a thing," I said.

"A . . . *Snork!* . . . thing?"

"A thingie thing."

Amanda gave me a suspicious look. I knew I had to distract her so I pointed at the clipboard. "What's that?"

"A petition." This was no surprise. At least once a week Amanda had some petition she wanted everyone to sign. "I've organized a new . . . *Snork!* . . . group called Students Against Unrealistic Body Images."

"SAUBI," I said.

"Huh?"

"It's the acronym for your new group," I explained.

"Whatever," said Amanda. "I just . . . *Snork!* . . . think it would be a really . . . *Snork!* . . . good gesture on your part to be the . . . *Snork!* . . . first to sign it."

Normally I didn't sign Amanda's petitions, but I was so eager to keep her distracted from the Mini-DITS that I took the clipboard. But before I

33

could sign it, we were suddenly surrounded by a group of kids, mostly sixth-grade girls.

"Did you meet her, Jake?" asked one.

"Did you get her autograph?" asked another.

"Was Angus with her?" a third asked.

Amanda turned on them. "How . . . *Snork!* . . . can you care about dumb things like that? Don't you realize you're . . . *Snork!* . . . all victims of a vast corporate and media plot to . . . *Snork!* . . . make women feel insecure about their body images?"

"What are you talking about?" one of the sixth-grade girls asked.

"Why are you making that weird sound?" asked another.

"Forget . . . *Snork!* . . . the sound," said Amanda. "I'm . . . *Snork!* . . . talking about how all these drug and cosmetic and clothing and weight-loss companies are . . . *Snork!* . . . trying to brainwash you into thinking you have to be thin and beautiful."

"You really ought to get your nose fixed," said one of the girls.

"Besides, we *want* to be thin and beautiful," said the second.

"We don't have to be brainwashed," the third said.

"But that's . . . *Snork!* . . . my point!" insisted Amanda. "The very . . . *Snork!* . . . fact that you want to be thin and beautiful means . . . *Snork!* . . . you've been brainwashed."

"Don't *you* want to be thin and beautiful?" one of the sixth-graders asked Amanda.

"Never!" Amanda replied in a huff.

"You're weird," one of them said.

"Definitely," agreed another.

"And you make funny sounds," added a third.

"But you only think that . . . *Snork!* . . . because you've been brainwashed," Amanda insisted.

"Okay, fine," the third said. "We've been brainwashed. Maybe we like being brainwashed." She turned to me. "So what's Lanny like?"

"I haven't met her yet," I said.

"Oh." All three girls looked disappointed. They turned to leave.

"But you haven't . . . *Snork!* . . . signed my petition," Amanda said.

"We can't," one said.

"We've been brainwashed," said the second.

"Get your nose fixed," added the third.

12

For the rest of the day I could hardly set foot in the hall or in a classroom without someone asking if I'd met Lanny Shanks. Even Principal Blanco asked. At the end of the school day I headed for my locker to dump some books. Josh and Andy were waiting for me.

"Ready?" Andy asked.

"For what?" I asked.

"To get Lanny's veggies," said Josh.

"Yeah, well, that's where I'm going," I said.

"Us, too," said Andy.

"Why?" I asked.

"We're your assistants," Andy announced.

"The assistants to the assistant," Josh said.

"You guys are sick," I mumbled.

"Then we're the sick assistants to the assistant," said Andy.

"Just call us the as*sick*tants," said Josh.

We left school and started down the sidewalk toward town.

"All I'm doing is going to buy vegetables, guys," I said.

"We know," said Andy.

"It's not exactly a big thrill," I said.

"It's okay," said Josh.

"Lanny's not going to be there," I said.

"Roger that," said Andy.

"You guys have never wanted to buy vegetables with me before," I said.

"We've changed," said Andy.

We kept walking. It didn't make sense. Why would Josh and Andy want to go shopping with me? Then I sensed something funny and looked back. About twenty yards behind us was a crowd of kids. When I stopped, they stopped.

"What's going on?" I asked my friends.

"I don't know," Josh answered.

"What are those kids doing?" I asked.

"What kids?" Andy asked.

I pointed. "*Those* kids, butt brain."

"Oh, *those* kids." Andy shrugged. "You got me."

"What kind of scam are you guys pulling?" I asked.

"Scam?" Josh repeated innocently. "Us? We don't know what you're talking about."

"Right." I didn't believe him for a second. "They just feel like following us for no reason."

"Stranger things have happened," Josh said.

At the supermarket I got a cart. Josh and Andy

stopped outside. The crowd of kids stopped about twenty feet away.

"Aren't you guys coming in?" I asked my friends.

"Naw, we'll wait out here," Andy said.

"I thought you wanted to go veggie shopping with me," I said.

"This is okay," said Josh.

That was fine with me. I went inside and headed for the fresh produce department. Shiela Shield had told me to get fresh carrots. Not the kind that came in a bag, but the kind that were bundled with a rubber band and had bushy green tops. I picked out a fresh-looking bundle. When I turned to put it in the cart, a girl was standing behind me.

"Could I have a tip of one of the carrots?" she asked.

"Uh, okay." I broke off an inch of carrot and gave it to her.

"Thanks a lot!" She turned and left.

Next I stopped to get lettuce. When I turned to put it in the cart, there was another girl behind me.

"Can I have a leaf of the lettuce?" she asked.

I gave her a leaf and she took off.

That's how it went the whole time I was in the store. Every time I turned around, another kid was waiting to get a little piece of whatever I'd

38

picked. And whether it was the green part of a strawberry or a leafy stalk of celery, they were totally thrilled.

Josh and Andy were still outside when I left the store. They both had big grins on their faces. The crowd of kids was gone. We started walking toward my house.

"Here you go, dude." Josh handed me a small wad of dollar bills.

"What's this?" I asked.

"Your cut," said Andy.

"My cut of what?" I asked.

"Your cut of 'Share a Meal with a Super-model,'" Josh explained. "Remember that crowd of kids? Each one of them now has a little piece of a meal with Lanny Shanks."

I looked down at the money in my hand and back at my friends. "You *charged them money* for those little pieces of carrots and lettuce?"

"Why not?" Josh asked.

"It wasn't like we twisted their arms," said Andy. "They wanted to pay us. They *begged* us."

I shoved the money back into Andy's hand. "You guys are crooks. I don't want any part of this."

Andy tried to give the money to me again. "Come on, Jake. Take your cut. We couldn't have done it without you."

"No."

"Come on," Andy tried again.

"Forget it, Andy," Josh said. "Jake doesn't want it."

"But it's not right," Andy argued.

"Maybe not," agreed Josh. "But we can't *force* him to take the money, can we?"

"Then what'll we do with it?" Andy asked.

"Aw, gee, Andy, let me think." Josh pretended to act dumb. "We could go find all those kids and give it back. Better yet, we could give it to charity. Hey! Wait! Here's a *really* crazy idea! We'll keep it ourselves!"

"But it's not right," Andy argued.

Josh rolled his eyes. "Okay, Andy, I see your point. Tell you what. I'll take the money. Then you won't have to worry about it anymore. How's that sound?"

Andy frowned. "On second thought, maybe we should split it."

Josh smirked. "Surprise, surprise."

13

At home I was putting the vegetables in the refrigerator when Jessica came into the kitchen.

"That's for Lanny?" she asked.

"Yeah." I closed the refrigerator door.

"How are you going to get to the mall at five o'clock in the morning?"

"Shiela Shield told me to take a cab," I said.

"You sure you can get a cab at that hour?"

"I don't know," I said. "I guess."

"If you can't get a cab, get me up and I'll take you," she said.

"I thought the last thing you wanted to do was be my personal chauffeur."

"Normally, that would be true," Jessica admitted. "But this isn't normal, Jake. How often do you get to work with a supermodel?"

"I thought you despised everything a supermodel stands for," I said.

"I do, Jake," she said. "But I'm not thinking of *her*. I'm thinking of *you*. This could be a huge opportunity."

"Opportunity for what?"

"For your future," she said. "For a career."

"A career as a supermodel's assistant?"

"No, but you might decide to become a photographer, or a makeup man, or a stylist."

"What's a stylist do?" I asked.

"Hair and clothes."

"Are you out of your mind? Why would I want a career in hair and clothes?"

"Okay, you're right, forget that." Jessica sighed. "So, I forgot what you said about the mini-thingie."

"The Mini-DITS?" I said. "What about it?"

"Oh, nothing." My sister started to look at a magazine.

I left the kitchen and went upstairs. Jessica wasn't making sense, but there was nothing particularly new about that. I went into my room and sat down on my bed. What a day! It seemed like *everyone* I knew was acting weird because of this supermodel thing.

I did my homework and had dinner and watched TV in the den. When I went back up to my room, I had a slightly weird feeling that things weren't quite the way I'd left them. Everything looked *almost* normal. All the drawers of my dresser were closed except the bottom one. But that was the one drawer I never went into. Maybe Jessica had been searching my room. Maybe not. One thing was certain. If I asked her, she was bound to deny it.

14

Rap! Rap! The sound of knocking on my door woke me. The room was dark. The red numerals on my radio alarm said 4:30. I rolled over and tried to go back to sleep.

Rap! Rap! "Jake?" It was Jessica.

"Go away," I moaned.

"You have to get up."

"It's the middle of the night. Go away."

"You're supposed to be at the mall in half an hour."

"Forget it. I quit." I rolled over and pulled the pillow over my head.

"What about Lanny's vegetables?"

"Let her come get them."

The next thing I knew, someone was shaking my shoulder. The lights in my room were on. The glare was horrible. I had to cover my eyes with my hand. "You have to get up, Jake. You have a responsibility. You accepted the job. Now you have to do it."

"I did it." I buried my head under the pillow again. "I bought the stupid vegetables. Leave me alone."

"No."

"Then why don't *you* bring her the stupid vegetables?" I suggested.

Jessica paused for a moment. I prayed she'd decide to do it and let me go back to sleep. But the next thing I knew, she started shaking my shoulder again. "It's your job and your responsibility, Jake. Come on, you're late. You don't even have time to call a cab. I'll have to drive you myself."

A little while later, still half asleep, I found myself sitting in the car with a big bag of cold vegetables on my lap.

"Are you nervous?" Jessica asked as we drove down the dark, empty streets.

"No, I'm tired." I yawned.

"Aren't you curious why they want you at the mall at five o'clock in the morning?"

"No." I closed my eyes and leaned back in the seat. I was just falling back to sleep when Jessica suddenly gasped. "Oh, wow!"

15

I opened my eyes. The mall parking lot looked like a night scene from the Old West with a bunch of covered wagons circled around a brightly glowing campfire. Only instead of covered wagons there were big trucks and motor homes. And instead of a campfire there were bright, glowing white-hot lights. Even though it was five in the morning, a lot of people were milling around.

"They must be shooting," Jessica said as she steered the car into the parking lot.

"Shooting who?" I yawned.

"Not *who*, *what*," Jessica said. "It's a photo shoot, Jake."

"Oh, right." Ahead of us in the headlight beams a police officer held up his hand. It was Officer Parsons of the Jeffersonville police. I knew him because he almost busted Andy in my dog Lance's body the time Andy and Lance switched.

Jessica rolled down her window. "Hey, Officer Parsons."

"Hi, Jessica. Hi, Jake," he said. "Sorry, but this is as far as you can go."

"How come?" my sister asked.

"They're doing some kind of photo shoot and the area is off-limits," Officer Parsons explained.

"But Jake's part of it." Jessica explained the contest I'd won. Officer Parsons told us to wait while he went back to his car and checked my name on the official list. A few moments later he was back.

"Okay, Jake," he said, leaning in the window. "You can go in."

"What about me?" my sister asked.

Officer Parsons shook his head. "Sorry, Jessica, they're really strict about who comes in."

Jessica frowned. "Well, okay, you better go, Jake."

"Thanks for the ride, Jess." I got out of the car with my bag of groceries.

"You know where you're supposed to go?" Officer Parsons asked.

"Not really," I said. "I'm supposed to bring these vegetables to Lanny Shanks."

"That's her trailer." Officer Parsons pointed at a long yellow motor home with a small gray satellite dish on top.

"That's not a trailer, it's a motor home," I said.

"I know," said the police officer. "But these folks call them trailers."

I carried the bag over to the motor home. The lights were on inside, but the shades were drawn, and I couldn't see in. In the front window was a sign that said: MIDDLE OF NOWHERE SHOOT.

I knocked on the door. A second later it was opened by a short blond woman. "Can I help you?"

I explained who I was and that I'd come bearing vegetables.

"Oh, great. Thanks." The blond woman took the bag of vegetables and started to close the door.

"Wait," I said.

"Yes?" said the blond woman.

I pointed at the sign in the window of the motor home. "Why's it say Middle of Nowhere Shoot?"

"That's just the name they gave it," she explained. "Every photo shoot has a name. Like London Night Life or Caribbean Beaches. It's, like, the theme."

"And this is the middle of nowhere?"

"Better believe it." The blond woman started to close the motor home door again.

"Wait!" I said. "What am I supposed to do now?"

"Whatever you like." Then she closed the door for good.

16

By the time I got to school that morning all I wanted to do was go back to sleep. I got out of the cab and found Andy and Josh waiting by the front entrance. Behind them in the school lobby was a big crowd of kids. Josh and Andy hurried toward me.

"How was it?" Josh asked eagerly.

"What's she like?" asked Andy.

"Why do you care?" I asked.

"Just tell us," Josh insisted.

"It was boring, and I have no idea what she's like," I answered with a yawn.

My friends frowned. "What do you mean?"

"I mean, I gave them the vegetables and then sat around for the whole rest of the time and didn't do a thing."

"But you met Lanny, right?" Andy asked.

I shook my head.

"You *sure* you didn't meet her?" Josh asked.

"I think I'd know if I met her, guys."

Josh and Andy traded a worried look and then glanced at the crowd of kids waiting in the school lobby.

Josh turned to me. "How do you feel about lying?"

"It'll be worth your while," Andy added. "We promise."

I rolled my eyes. "What scam are you guys up to this time?"

Josh and Andy shared a guilty look.

"See all those kids in the lobby?" Josh said. "Each one of them has already paid to meet someone who knows Lanny Shanks."

"If you don't tell them you met her we're gonna have to give all the money back," Andy said.

I shook my head. "Tough luck."

"Come on, Jake," Andy begged. "We're talking about a lot of money."

"No way, guys," I said. "Either you tell them I didn't meet her or I will. Either way you're giving back the money."

"Gee, thanks, Jake," grumbled Andy.

"Yeah," added Josh. "Some friend."

With hanging heads they went back to the school lobby and gave everyone their money back.

Another crowd of kids was waiting for me in homeroom, but these were mostly my friends and they hadn't paid Andy or Josh anything. When I entered the room, they looked at me with excited, hopeful expressions.

"Forget it, guys," Josh announced. "He didn't even meet her."

Around the room faces fell. I could see disappointment in everyone's eyes.

"Did you at least *see* her?" asked Amber.

"Oh, yeah, I saw her," I said.

All around the room faces brightened again.

"Was she really . . . *Snork!* . . . pushy and demanding?" asked Amanda.

"Did she insist that everyone treat her like a star?" asked Alex Silver.

"Did she want M&Ms with all the green ones taken out?" asked Barry Dunn.

I stared at him. "What?"

Barry shrugged. "I heard that some star asked for that."

"Actually she seemed really sweet and nice to everyone," I said. "It was almost weird. Like all these people would crowd around her fixing her hair and makeup and her clothes and she'd just stand there and let them do anything they liked."

"What about when she was modeling?" asked Amber.

"Same thing," I said. "She did whatever the photographer told her to do and never said anything."

"She must have noticed you," said Julia.

"No way," I said. "She doesn't even know I exist."

Everyone looked pretty disappointed. Around the room kids turned back to their homework or started talking with friends. Suddenly I was no big deal.

Then the PA system blared on. "Jake Sherman, to the office immediately."

17

If you thought my friends were disappointed, you should have seen Principal Blanco.

"You didn't get the poster signed?" The corners of his mouth turned down into a sad frown. We were sitting in his office. The door was shut.

"I couldn't get close to her," I said, although the real truth was that I'd totally forgotten to bring the poster in the first place.

"But you gave me your word," he said.

"I'm supposed to go back tonight," I said. "I'll try to get her to sign it then. I promise!"

Principal Blanco gazed down at his desk and ran his fingers through his curly black hair. "Jake, I . . . I'm not sure you understand what this means to me. This is a dream come true. I mean, Lanny Shanks . . . here in Jeffersonville. I . . . Jake, please, you must get that poster signed. You must! Simply *trying* isn't good enough. You must *do* it!"

"I'll do it," I said. "I promise."

Principal Blanco nodded without looking at me. "Thank you, Jake. Now go and Godspeed. Accomplish your mission!"

I left the office and went to class. Word that I hadn't met Lanny Shanks must have spread around the school fast because no one stopped me in the hall or asked me any questions.

At lunch Andy and Josh sat at our regular table with glum expressions on their faces.

"What's with you guys?" I asked.

Neither said a word. They just slowly chewed their hamburgers.

"Come on, tell me," I said.

"We lost a lot of money," Josh said.

"How?" I asked.

"This morning," he said. "We had to pay all those kids back."

"You didn't *lose* that money," I said. "It wasn't yours to begin with. You just gave it back to the people it belonged to."

Josh shrugged. "Well, it *feels* like we lost a lot of money, okay?"

"You're acting like it's my fault," I said. "I never told you to charge kids money because you thought I was going to meet Lanny Shanks."

Josh stared down at his lunch and didn't say a thing.

"It's not just that," mumbled Andy. "We had a shot at being famous."

"No, you didn't," I said.

"Well, *semifamous*, at least."

"Bull," I said. "You don't get famous just because you *know* someone who might *meet* someone famous."

"You do around here," Josh pointed out.

"That's so bogus," I said. "You get famous because you do something that makes you famous. Not because of who you know."

"So you're not going back, right?" Andy asked. "I mean, what's the point if you don't get to meet Lanny?"

"But I agreed to do it," I said.

"You were misled, dude," Josh said. "They made you think you were gonna meet the hottest babe in the world. Instead you're just buying her vegetables. If I were you I'd blow the whole thing off."

"Yeah," Andy agreed. "It's not like they're gonna miss you if you don't show up."

They were probably right. Winning the contest was a joke. They wouldn't even notice if I didn't show up that afternoon. Besides, I'd been up since 4:30 in the morning and I was really tired.

Just then Principal Blanco came into the cafetorium. He didn't even say anything to me. He just gave me a look. I knew if I didn't get Lanny Shanks to sign that poster, I was dead meat.

18

By the time school ended, I just wanted to go home and take a nap. But I had to get that poster signed, so I caught a cab over to the mall. When I got to the part of the parking lot where the trailers were, no one was around. One of the truck drivers was sitting in his truck, reading the paper.

"Uh, excuse me," I said. "Where'd everyone go?"

"They're over at some park shooting," the truck driver said. "They'll be back later."

It must have been Jeffersonville Park. I wondered if I should go over there, but I knew I'd wind up standing around doing nothing. I'd never be able to get close enough to Lanny to get her to sign the poster. Just then the door to Lanny's trailer opened and a stocky woman with short black hair and all black clothes came out.

"Who are you?" she demanded.

"I, er, won this contest," I started to explain. "The assistant to the super — "

"Right, I spoke to you," the woman said. "I'm Shiela Shield, Lanny's personal secretary. Come in here, I need you."

I went over to the trailer and climbed in. The inside of the trailer looked like equal parts make-up room, closet, kitchenette, and living room. It had a couch and a TV, a table with a big mirror and tons of makeup, and racks of dresses all over the place. The whole trailer smelled like perfume.

Shiela Shield handed me a plastic bucket. In it were some rags and bottles of Windex and Fantastik.

"Clean up this pigsty," she ordered. "Do the bathroom in the back. Polish the mirrors. I want this place looking shipshape when Lanny comes back."

"But — "

"No buts," Shiela Shield snapped. "You wanted this job, now get to work."

Shiela marched out of the trailer and slammed the door behind her. I looked down at the bucket. Somehow I'd gone from vegetable buyer to cleaning boy. The truth was, I *didn't* want the job. I'd *never* wanted it. But now it looked like I was stuck with it until I got that poster signed.

The good news was the trailer had satellite TV so at least I'd have some fun while I cleaned.

By the time I finished, I was pretty wiped out. That couch in front of the satellite TV was starting to look really good. I figured it couldn't hurt to sit down and just zone out for a few minutes.

19

"What have we here?" a voice asked.

I opened my eyes. Standing over me was a tall, extremely thin woman with blond hair. She was wearing sunglasses, which seemed kind of strange considering it was dark outside.

"Where am I?" I asked.

"You're in my trailer," she answered.

I rubbed my eyes. "Who are you?"

"I think the correct question is, Who are *you*? And what are you doing in my trailer?"

"I won this contest to be Lanny Shanks's personal assistant," I said with a yawn. "And so far my job has been to buy her vegetables and clean up her trailer."

"Haaaa!" The tall, very thin lady laughed loudly. "You had to win a contest to get to do that?"

"I know, it sounds kind of dumb," I admitted.

The woman in the sunglasses looked around the trailer. "You did a good job."

"Thanks." I got up and stretched. "Know what time it is?"

"Around nine," she said.

"Oh, wow, guess I better get going," I said.

"But aren't you supposed to be Lanny Shanks's personal assistant?" she asked.

"It's totally bogus," I said. "They're never gonna let me meet her."

"What makes you think that?" she asked.

"It's just the way it is. She's famous and important. She's a somebody and I'm a nobody. And the way things work in this world, the nobodies don't get to meet the somebodies."

The tall, very thin lady smiled softly, revealing some of the straightest and whitest teeth I'd ever seen. She took off her sunglasses. "They do now."

20

I'm not sure Lanny Shanks was quite as beautiful in person as she was on all those magazine covers. But she sure came close. It was hard to take my eyes off her. Waves of goose bumps washed up and down my arms.

"You're staring," she said.

"Sorry." I quickly turned my gaze to the floor.

"You don't have to apologize," she said. "I'm used to it."

Lanny sat down at the makeup table and started to use round white pads to wipe the makeup off her face.

"You sure you don't want me to go?" I asked. "I mean, you must be kind of tired. It's been a long day."

"I took a nap," she said as she wiped her chin and cheeks. "I try to avoid the sun. It's terrible for the skin. Be a dear and scoop the avocados into a bowl, will you?"

"All of them?"

"Yes."

I knew there were fifty avocados because I'd bought them at the supermarket the day before. If Lanny wanted all fifty, she must have been *way* hungry. I went into the kitchenette and got to work scooping them into this big metal bowl. I was so busy that I didn't even realize that Lanny had gotten up from the makeup table and changed clothes.

The next time I looked up, she was standing next to the couch, wearing a tiny white terry cloth robe that stopped about one-third of the way down her thighs. Her long legs were bare. I felt my face grow hot with embarrassment. This was one aspect of being her personal assistant that I'd never considered.

"Did you mash up the avocados?" she asked.

"Uh, I will." I picked up a masher and started to mash, aware that it was now Lanny's turn to stare at me.

"Are you all right?" she asked.

"Oh, sure. Why do you ask?"

"Your face is all red."

"Oh, uh . . . mashing these avocados is hard work," I lied.

"When you're finished, bring it over here," she said.

"You want some crackers with it?" I asked.

"No, silly, I'm not going to eat it."

Not eat it? Then what was she going to do with it? I picked up the bowl of mashed avocados and turned to bring it to Lanny.

She was still standing next to the couch. Only now she was no longer wearing that little robe.

21

I instantly spun around so my back was facing her.

"I'm over here, silly," she said behind me.

"I know." I started to walk toward her, backward.

"If you walk like that there's a good chance you'll fall," she said.

"I'll be careful."

"It would be easier if you turned around."

"This is okay."

"What's your name again?" Lanny asked.

"Jake."

"Jake, you really don't have to be embarrassed. I'm used to people seeing me undressed. I spend half my life undressing in front of people."

"I, er, uh . . ."

"And it's not like I'm *completely* undressed," she said.

As I walked backward I glanced out of the

corner of my eye at the mirror on the makeup table. What I thought was Lanny's underwear now appeared to be a skimpy bikini bathing suit.

"Have you ever been to the beach, Jake?" Lanny asked.

"Yes," I answered with my back to her.

"Have you ever seen a woman in a bathing suit?"

"Yes."

"So?"

"So this isn't the beach and that's not much of a bathing suit."

"Ha!" Lanny laughed again. "You're funny, Jake. Now put down the bowl and get a couple of big sheets of plastic wrap from the roll."

Keeping my eyes averted, I handed the bowl of mashed avocado to Lanny and went back into the kitchenette. Next to the counter was a superwide roll of plastic wrap, like the kind you can buy in a warehouse store.

"How big?" I asked.

"Four sheets, each one about seven feet long," Lanny answered.

I did as I was told.

"Good," Lanny said after I was finished. "Now put two of the sheets on the couch lengthwise."

Again I did as I was told.

"Great." Lanny put down the bowl of avocado mush and laid down on the couch on top of the long sheets of plastic wrap.

"Can I ask what we're doing?" I asked.

"Sure," answered Lanny. "You're putting me to bed."

22

Every night Lanny Shanks turned herself into a plastic-coated avocado-mush wrap sandwich. After she slathered herself in avocado mush, my job was to put the other plastic sheets on top of her and then tuck in the sides so the mush wouldn't leak out onto the couch. Next I had to cover her eyes with slices of cucumber. Lanny Shanks might have been a vegetarian, but she *wore* more vegetables than she ate.

"All I need now is my disk player," Lanny said, with cucumber slices on her eyes.

"I thought you were going to sleep," I said.

"No, I'm just resting," she replied. "Angus is coming by later."

I found her disk player and put the headphones on her and pushed the play button.

"Louder, please," Lanny said.

I turned up the volume.

"That's good, thank you. You can go now."

I stared down at Lanny Shanks, looking avocado green inside her clear plastic wrap, cucumber slices on her eyes, and headphones blasting. Now that my job was done, I went into the bathroom at the back of the trailer and washed the avocado mush off my hands. The funny thing was, if I ever told my friends about meeting Lanny and helping turn her into a clear plastic avocado wrap, they probably would be thrilled.

But I decided I wouldn't tell them.

I dried my hands and left the bathroom.

That's when things really got weird.

Amanda Gluck was in the trailer.

And she had the Mini-DITS!

23

The Mini-DITS had two headsets. Amanda was already wearing one on her own head, and she was leaning over Lanny with the other. It didn't take a genius to figure out what she was trying to do.

"Stop!" I hissed as loudly as I dared without bothering Lanny.

When Amanda saw me come out of the bathroom, she lunged toward Lanny in a last desperate attempt to put the Mini-DITS headset on her.

I got there just in time to grab the headset away. Amanda put her head down and charged me like a bull. She head-butted me backward into the dress rack. As I fell, I accidentally yanked a dozen dresses off their hangers. The Mini-DITS fell to the floor of the trailer. Amanda picked it up and turned back toward Lanny.

Still tangled in dresses, I lurched forward and grabbed the back of Amanda's T-shirt. That slowed her down but didn't stop her. Like a dog pulling a heavy sled she started to huff and puff and drag me toward Lanny.

I couldn't get to my feet because they were tangled in dresses. Amanda kept pulling. I held on tight and felt myself sliding along the trailer floor.

Just as Amanda was about to reach Lanny, I let go of the T-shirt. Amanda shot forward like a slingshot and crashed into a rack of clothes.

"Wha?" In her clear plastic avocado-mush wrap, Lanny stirred. Amanda and I both froze. I was on my hands and knees with my feet still tangled in dresses. Amanda was halfway out of the dress rack she'd fallen into.

"Jake?" Lanny called. "Are you still here?"

"Yes," I said.

Without moving the cucumbers from her eyes or the earphones from her head, she asked, "Did something fall? I thought I heard a crash."

I looked at Amanda and back at Lanny. "It was just a mouse. Er, I mean, a rat."

"Can you get it out of here?" Lanny asked calmly. She was one cool character. Nothing seemed to faze her.

"Definitely," I replied.

I turned to Amanda and pointed at the trailer door. Amanda shook her head stubbornly. She climbed out of the dress rack and started toward Lanny. She still had the Mini-DITS. I was the only thing between supernerd and supermodel.

And my feet were still tangled in dresses.

Amanda faked right and went left. Once again I managed to grab her shirt. The next thing I knew, she was dragging me toward Lanny again.

And then the trailer door opened.

24

It was Jessica.

"What in the world?" she gasped when she saw Amanda dragging me toward Lanny. Amanda and I both turned and pressed our fingers to our lips and went *shush*!

Jessica made a face. I pointed at Amanda and the Mini-DITS. My sister's eyes went wide as she realized what was happening.

I quickly mouthed the words "Help me get her out of here!"

Jessica rushed over and held Amanda. That gave me time to untangle the dresses around my ankles. Then, with each of us holding one of Amanda's arms, we started to pull her away. Even with the two of us pulling, I couldn't believe how strong Amanda was. Or maybe it was just how badly she wanted to switch bodies with Lanny Shanks.

Finally, we managed to get Amanda through the door of the trailer and outside.

"What are you doing here?" I asked my sister as we dragged Amanda away from the trailer.

"Mom sent me over because it was late and she was worried about you," Jessica answered. "You keep Amanda out here. I'll go back and straighten up the clothes that fell over."

Once we'd gotten Amanda outside, she stopped fighting so hard. I guess she realized that it was two against one and she wasn't going to win. We stood in the dark and straightened our clothes.

"How'd you know about the Mini-DITS?" I asked.

"Oh, come on, Jake," Amanda said. "It wasn't hard to figure out. I knew there was something you used. Then that day at your locker you acted so guilty. I put two and two together."

"I thought you were totally against models," I said.

"I am," Amanda replied.

"Then why were you trying so hard to switch?"

"I wanted to understand what it was like," Amanda explained. "You know the saying 'Know thine enemy'?"

"Sure," I said. "I've heard of '*Know* thine enemy.' I've just never heard of *be* thine enemy. Now, how about getting thine butt out of here?"

Under the parking lot lights Amanda's eyes started to well up with tears and her lips turned into a big pouty frown. "This is so unfair!"

"What is?" I asked.

"Nothing *you'll* ever understand!" She got on her bike and rode off into the dark. I looked back at the trailer. Suddenly I realized Jessica was still inside. It seemed like she was taking an awful long time just to pick up some clothes from the floor.

25

I went back into the trailer. Jessica was down by the couch, leaning over Lanny. Now my sister was wearing one of the headsets from the Mini-DITS.

And that could only mean one thing!

I practically dove the length of the trailer and yanked the headset off Jessica. She tried to grab it back. I'm not sure exactly what happened next, but somehow the second headset got tangled with the earphones for Lanny's portable disc player.

And the red button on the Mini-DITS got pushed.

And there was a loud *whump*!

And that's when things *really* got weird.

26

Thanks to the Mini-DITS and its big brother, the DITS, I've switched bodies with a lot of people. Sometimes when I wake up I'm not sure at first if I've really switched. The air gets hazy, I'm kind of dazed, and it's hard to tell what's going on.

But this time I knew instantly.

Because I was lying on the couch, encased in a clear plastic avocado-mush wrap. Imagine feeling warm and slimy from your head to your toes, not to mention being wrapped up like a mummy.

Meanwhile, Lanny in my body was sitting on the floor looking dazed. Jessica was standing in between us. Her eyes were darting back and forth frantically.

"Jake?" she said.

"You're looking at him, I mean, her," I said in Lanny's avocado-wrapped body.

"Would someone care to tell me what's going on?" Lanny Shanks in my body asked calmly.

"Ms. Shanks?" Jessica's mouth fell open.

Lanny nodded my head. "Call me Lanny."

"Oh, my gosh, Lanny, I'm so sorry! There's been a terrible mistake. You see, you're not supposed to be in my brother's body. You're supposed to, er, be in . . ." Her voice trailed off.

"In what?" Lanny sounded genuinely curious.

Jessica stared at the supermodel in my body. "How can you be so calm about this?"

"About being in this body instead of my own?" Lanny in my body asked.

Jessica nodded.

"Oh, I don't know," said Lanny in my body. "I guess it's what happens when you spend your whole life being treated like you're only a body. So now this is just another body. No big deal. I was sort of getting bored with mine anyway."

Jessica stared at me in Lanny's body and then back at Lanny in my body.

"You mean, if I'd walked up to you and said I wanted to switch bodies with you, you would have agreed?" my sister asked.

Lanny in my body frowned. "No offense or anything, but why would I want to go from my body to yours?"

"Why would you want to go from your body to my brother's scuzzy body?" Jessica asked back.

"I didn't," Lanny replied, "but now that the deed's done, it's kind of a kick to be in a boy's body."

"Right!" I pumped Lanny's fist.

"Why?" Jessica asked.

"Well, I can probably go for days without taking a shower," said Lanny in my body. "I don't have to wash my hair, or do my nails, or put on makeup. I can play ball without worrying about chipping a nail. I don't have to worry about going out in the sun and — " Lanny in my body looked down at me in hers. "I won't have to spend every night wrapped in that disgusting slime and feeling like I belong on the sandwich counter of some health food store."

"But you won't be famous or rich," Jessica stammered.

"Hon, I've *been* famous and I *am* rich," Lanny in my body replied. "And believe me, neither is much good if it means you can't go out and have fun."

Lanny in my body bent down and picked up the Mini-DITS. "Is this the thing that did it?"

I nodded Lanny's head.

"Can I assume that when the time comes we can use it to switch back?" asked Lanny in my body.

"Probably," I answered in her body. "And if that one doesn't work, there's another one."

"A backup body-switching machine? How responsible of you." Lanny in my body tucked the Mini-DITS under her arm. "I think I'll hold on to this one anyway."

Vaarrrrrooooommmmmm! From outside came the smooth, high-pitched whine of an expensive sports car. Lanny in my body went over to the trailer window and squinted outside. A smile appeared on my face. "Well, well, look who's here."

Lanny in my body turned to me in hers. "Have fun with Angus, Jake." Next, she turned to Jessica and slid my arm through my sister's. "Come on, sis, let's go."

Lanny in my body and Jessica headed toward the trailer door. Just as they were about to leave, Lanny in my body paused and looked back at me in hers. "One last thing, Jake."

"What?" I asked from the couch where I was still in the avocado wrap.

"It's been weeks since Angus and I have seen each other," said Lanny in my body. "Don't do anything I wouldn't do."

27

Jessica and Lanny in my body left the trailer and closed the door behind them. I would have done just about anything to get out of there. Unfortunately I was wrapped in plastic. A moment later the trailer door opened and Angus Bangus, the lead singer of Power Strum, strolled in.

Angus was built more like a football player than a rock star. He was big and broad-shouldered with a shaved head and lots of earrings and tattoos. He was wearing heavy black leather shoes, baggy pants, and a sleeveless black T-shirt that showed off his muscular arms and tattoos. With each step he took, the whole trailer shook. He looked exactly like the kind of person you did not want to be alone with.

Angus stopped beside the couch and looked down at me in Lanny's body. He didn't even blink. He acted like seeing his girlfriend wrapped in green slime and plastic was an everyday thing.

"Who was that?" he asked.

"The two girls?" I said in Lanny's body.

Angus scowled. "Not two girls. A guy and a girl."

Oops! He was right. I had to remember whose body I was in, and who was in my body.

"Just friends," I said in Lanny's body.

"Friends? How come I never seen them before?"

"New friends."

"*New* friends?" Angus was one of those people who repeated everything you said but turned it into a question.

"The boy won the assistant to a supermodel contest," I explained. "The girl's his sister."

Angus narrowed one eye suspiciously. "That kid don't spend any time alone in here with you, does he?"

I got the feeling that Angus was the jealous type.

"He's just a kid," I replied in Lanny's body.

"Yeah, but not bad looking," said Angus, who was obviously a man with excellent taste. "So why don't you get out of that stuff and we'll go out."

"Now?" A clock on the makeup table said it was after eleven P.M.

"Too early?" asked Angus.

"Too late?" I said in Lanny's body.

Angus frowned. "What's with you?"

Apparently Angus and Lanny were night owls.

"Come on, Lanny, let's get out of here," Angus said. "I'm hungry."

The words had hardly left Angus's lips when I became aware of a sensation coming from inside Lanny's body. Her stomach was grumbling and churning. She wasn't just hungry, she was starving. It felt like she hadn't eaten in a week!

On the other hand, eating meant going out with Angus.

And that was enough to make anyone lose their appetite!

"So?" said Angus.

Lanny's stomach was so empty it hurt. I decided to take my chances. "Could you help me out of this?"

"Sure." Angus bent down and unpeeled the plastic.

As soon as I could move Lanny's arms and legs, I sat up. "Okay, thanks, you can go now."

Angus frowned. "Go?"

"Er, uh, stay, but don't touch." I swiveled around and got up.

"What's with you?" Angus asked.

"I'm feeling slimy." In Lanny's body, I hurried to the bathroom. It was a relief to lock the door and get into the shower. Lanny may have joked about not having to take a shower in my body, but in her body I lathered and scrubbed every inch to get that avocado slime off me. Then I shampooed her hair and rinsed.

It felt really good until I realized I had another problem. I had no clothes to put on.

28

Lanny's fingers and toes were starting to get that pruney look when Angus finally knocked on the bathroom door.

"Hey, Lanny, come on, let's book."

"Just a minute," I called from the shower.

"You've already had half an hour," he complained.

I would have stayed for another half hour, but suddenly the shower stopped. I realized I must have used up all the water in the trailer's water tank.

In Lanny's body I got out of the shower and started to towel off. It was time to face the next problem.

"Angus?" I called through the bathroom door.

"Yeah?"

"Could you get me some clothes?"

"Sure, what do you want?"

"Jeans and a T-shirt."

A moment later he knocked on the door. "Here you go."

"Just leave them by the door," I called from inside.

"Huh?" Angus said. "Open the door and I'll give them to you."

"No."

"What's with you?" Angus asked. I was starting to get the feeling that this was a question he asked a lot.

"I'm feeling shy," I said through the door.

"You?" Angus sounded surprised. "Since when?"

"Please?" I asked.

"Oh, okay."

I heard the sound of Angus's footsteps heading away from the door. I quickly opened it. A white T-shirt and jeans were lying on the floor. I grabbed them and closed the door again.

It was easy to get the T-shirt on, but I'd never seen a pair of jeans like those. They looked like they were about a foot too long, and they were so tight that even for a string bean like Lanny I thought I'd never get them on.

Finally, by sucking in Lanny's stomach and holding her breath, I managed to zip up the jeans and close them.

When I left the bathroom, Angus was sitting on the couch, watching satellite TV. He looked up at me and scowled. "You're going out like that?"

"Why not?"

"Your hair," he said.

"I washed it."

"Yeah, I can see that," said Angus. "But you never go out unless it's all blow-dried and brushed and perfect. And how come you're not wearing makeup?"

"Don't feel like it."

Angus frowned. You could see he was a big frowner. But he turned off the TV and got up. I followed him out of the trailer.

"Whoa!" Parked outside in the dark was a red Ferrari Superrossa convertible.

"What?" Angus asked.

"Nice wheels."

"You *like* it?" Angus asked, puzzled.

"What's not to like?" I asked, running Lanny's fingers over the glossy paint.

"Wow, I don't know what's gotten into you, Lanny," Angus said as he held the door open for me. "You used to hate this car. You said only insecure rich guys drove them."

"You must be thinking of someone else." In Lanny's body I slid down into the car's soft tan leather seats.

Angus got into the driver's seat. "So what do you feel like?"

"Going really fast. High-speed cornering. Maybe popping a few wheelies."

Angus scowled at me again. "I meant, in terms of food."

"Oh, uh, how about pizza?"

Angus kept scowling. I wanted to warn him that if he didn't change his expression soon he might get stuck that way permanently. "Since when do you like pizza?"

"Since when do you ask so many questions?"

Angus shrugged and started the Ferrari. *Vaarrrrooooommmmmm!* The engine revved and settled down into a purr. The next thing I knew, we were racing through the night with the wind blowing through my, I mean, through Lanny's damp hair.

29

Now, girls, in case you're wondering what it's like to be a supermodel and drive around Jeffersonville at night in a convertible Ferrari with a famous rock star, here's your answer:

No one noticed!

Maybe everyone in Jeffersonville is brain dead. Or maybe people noticed and thought to themselves, *Gee, that looks just like supermodel Lanny Shanks and rock star Angus Bangus in a Ferrari. Wait, this is Jeffersonville. So that's impossible.*

More likely, no one noticed because when Lanny sat in a car with wet, stringy hair and no makeup, she didn't look like Lanny.

Anyway, we got to the Slice of Life pizzeria, which is the only place in Jeffersonville open after midnight. Angus parked the Ferrari out in front and looked in with yet another scowl.

"You sure about this, Lanny?" he asked.

"What's wrong?"

"Looks kind of grubby in there."

I wasn't sure what he was talking about. To me, the Slice of Life looked like your basic pizzeria. It had chairs and tables and a counter where you got your slices. There might have been a couple of flies buzzing around, and the tables were sometimes greasy, but what pizzeria didn't have that?

Besides, in Lanny's body I was so hungry, I didn't care where we ate. The scent of freshly baked pizza wafted into Lanny's nose, and the next thing I knew, I was out of the Ferrari and inside.

The Slice of Life didn't have waiters. You went up to the counter and ordered.

"I'll have a pizza with sausage, pepperoni, and meatballs," I told the guy in the stained white T-shirt behind the counter.

Angus frowned, then almost grinned. "You're joking, right?"

"No."

"What about the Pledge of Veg?" Angus asked.

"The Pledge of Veg was just a hedge," I said in Lanny's body.

"A hedge against what?"

I shrugged Lanny's shoulders and turned to the counter guy. "Got any Zoom?"

"Twenty-four-ounce bottles only," he said.

"I'll take one."

Angus looked horrified. "Isn't that the stuff

with five times the caffeine and four times the sugar?"

"Yes," I said in Lanny's body. "It's the best."

Angus shook his head in disbelief. "What's gotten into you?"

"Girls just want to have fun." I flashed him Lanny's brightest smile.

Angus looked pale. He ordered a small veggie pie and bottled water. I blew some great saliva bubbles while we waited. Oddly, Lanny's saliva was perfect and bubble after bubble floated off her tongue.

Angus watched silently. He hardly said a thing, while I, in Lanny's body, wolfed down my sausage, pepperoni, and meatball pie and finished off all twenty-four ounces of Zoom.

It must have been two A.M. when we got back to the trailer. Angus parked the Ferrari and sat staring at me in Lanny's body.

Suddenly I had a terrifying thought. Was he waiting for me to invite him in?

30

Nervous shivers ran up and down Lanny's arms. Angus didn't say a word. He just kept staring at me.

"Is something wrong?" I asked in Lanny's body.

"Do you have to ask?" Angus replied. "Of course something's wrong."

I slid Lanny's hand down to the door handle in case I had to make a fast exit.

"This is a message, isn't it?" Angus asked.

"What do you mean?"

"You're too smart to play dumb, Lanny," Angus said. "You know *exactly* what I mean. This is your way of telling me we're through. Going out without makeup. Blowing spit bubbles. Renouncing the Pledge of Veg." He paused and let out a deep, trembling sigh. "You've gone back to being a . . . carnivore."

Angus could hardly get the word out without choking. It sounded familiar, but I couldn't quite place it at that moment. "Remind me what a carnivore is?"

"An animal that eats meat."

"Oh, right." Now I remembered. "And a herbivore eats plants. And an omnivore eats omnis."

Angus scowled. "What is *with* you?"

"Lighten up, Angus, it was a joke."

"This just isn't like you," Angus said. "Tell me the truth, Lanny, have you met someone else?"

31

Looking back on it now, what I did next was probably a major mistake. But at the time it seemed to make a lot of sense. If I told Angus I'd met someone else, then he'd understand that I wasn't interested in him anymore and I wouldn't have to worry about him wanting to come into the trailer.

"Yes, Angus," I said, in Lanny's body. "I have."

Angus's eyes glistened like a sad puppy dog's. "Who?"

"You don't know him."

His eyes narrowed. "Don't lie to me. I know everyone you know, Lanny."

Uh-oh! "This is someone new."

"Someone from around here?" Angus asked.

It hadn't occurred to me, but why not? "Yes."

Angus leaned toward me and looked right into Lanny's eyes. "Tell me who, Lanny. I promise I won't do nothing. But I just have to know."

I had to make up someone fast. Who did I know who was old enough for Lanny? Who would it even make sense to name? The answer came in a flash.

"He's a principal. At a nearby middle school."

32

It was sad. With his head hanging, Angus drove slowly out of the mall parking lot. I sort of hoped he'd get all dramatic and pop a wheelie and leave a couple of hundred yards of rubber, but no such luck.

I couldn't have gotten more than a few hours' sleep before there was a knock on the trailer door. Outside was Stephanie, the blond woman who'd taken the bag of groceries from me the day before. It turned out that she was Lanny's personal makeup artist. She was followed by Kelly, who did Lanny's hair, and Barb, who handled her wardrobe.

For the next few hours I either sat or stood and let them work on Lanny's body, face, and hair. Then it was time for the shoot. Today the Middle of Nowhere shoot called for Lanny to model high heels, jeans, and an almost see-through blouse while standing in line with a bunch of local folks to see a movie. They purposely picked people who were kind of short so that in the high heels Lanny towered over them.

In Lanny's body I think I faked it pretty well. The only real problem came when I had to walk in those high heels. Imagine using stilts while standing on your tiptoes. Finally I had a real brainstorm. When it was time to walk, I took the high heels off. When it was time to pose, I put them back on.

The shoot lasted until around eleven in the morning. Then, from the things people said, I got the impression that it was time for Lanny to take her daily nap. It sounded good to me, so I headed back to the trailer.

I'd just gotten inside when there was a knock on the trailer door. I assumed it was Stephanie, Kelly, or Barb but when I looked out the window, I saw Josh and Andy.

I went to the door and opened it. "What are you guys doing here?"

Neither Josh nor Andy said a word. They couldn't take their eyes off me in Lanny's body.

"Is that really *you*, Jake?" Josh sounded awed.

"Who else?"

"You are such a babe!" Andy said.

"Thanks. So what's up? Shouldn't you be at school? How'd you get past Officer Parsons?"

Josh nodded his head off to the left. In Lanny's

body, I leaned out of the trailer. Jessica was busy gabbing to the police officer.

"We snuck out and Jessica brought us over," Andy explained. "You have a problem, Jake. You know how Lanny Shanks is in your body? Well, she's giving all the girls in school diet and fashion tips."

"It's seriously embarrassing," said Josh.

"People are starting to wonder about you, Jake," added Andy.

"As your best friends, we feel it is our responsibility to save your reputation," said Josh.

"I appreciate it, guys." In Lanny's body I left the trailer. "Let's go."

33

If walking in high heels isn't easy, neither is being a model and getting into a small car. There may be a lot of six-foot-tall people in the world, but few of them have legs as long as Lanny's. In Lanny's body I sat in the front seat while Josh and Andy got in the back. Jessica got into the driver's seat, but instead of starting the car, she turned and stared at me in Lanny's body.

"What?" I asked.

"Sorry," Jessica said. "I just can't believe Lanny Shanks is sitting in our car."

"Take a picture. I'll even pose."

"Believe me," said my sister. "If I had a camera, I *would* take a picture."

We started to drive. Lanny's knees were pressed painfully against the dashboard. I slid the seat back.

"Hey!" Andy yelled. "You're crushing my legs!"

"I can't help it," I said in Lanny's body. "It's either yours or mine."

"So why should it be mine?" Andy asked.

"Because Lanny's legs are famous and yours aren't," said Josh. "She *needs* hers."

"What?" Andy huffed. "I don't need mine?"

"Not as much as Lanny needs hers," Jessica said.

We stopped at a light.

"Uh, Jake?" Josh said from the back.

"What?" I said in Lanny's body.

"Look at the car next to us."

I looked to my right. Two young women in the car next to us were both staring at me in Lanny Shanks's body. Their lips were moving and you could see that they were saying "Lanny Shanks?"

In Lanny's body I smiled and waved. The light turned green and Jessica started to drive.

"Guess what?" Josh said. "They're following us. And one of them is on a cell phone."

A minute later a dark green SUV screeched around a corner and pulled up beside us. Two new women inside stared at me. They were both on cell phones.

From then on, new cars arrived at practically every corner and followed us. Andy looked out the back window.

"That makes six," said Josh.

"The red sports car makes seven," Andy corrected him. He leaned back in his seat and put his hands behind his head. "Seven cars of babes following us. I'm starting to like this."

"Reality check, Andy," said my sister. "They're not following *you*."

By the time we got to Burp It Up Middle School, the line of cars had increased to more than a dozen. We drove through the gates and the whole line followed. Jessica parked in front of the main doors. Some kids hanging around in the lobby glanced outside, probably wondering why all the cars were there.

"Wait a minute," said Josh in the backseat. "Am I the only one who thinks this is crazy?"

"You mean, letting Lanny walk into school?" Jessica guessed.

"You'll get mobbed," Josh said to me in Lanny's body.

"Too late," said Andy.

All those women from the cars that had followed us were getting out and running toward my sister's car.

"Lock the doors!" Jessica cried.

34

The crowd of women surrounded our car and started banging on the windows and yelling Lanny's name.

"This is seriously weird," Josh groaned.

"They're going to break the car!" Jessica cried.

"Hit the horn," I said in Lanny's body.

Jessica pressed down on the horn. The women outside the car jumped back in surprise, but a second later they were once again beating on the car and screaming Lanny's name.

"Any other brilliant ideas, Jake?" Josh asked with a smirk.

"Hey, I don't see *you* coming up with any great ideas," I shot back.

But now a new voice joined the fray. "Get back! Everyone back! This is school property! You are trespassing. Leave at once or I'll call the police!"

It was Principal Blanco, fighting his way through the crowd. The threat of calling the police seemed to work. The women began to back away. Of course, Principal Blanco didn't realize why they'd all crowded around Jessica's car in the first place. All he knew was that the women weren't supposed to be on school property.

Finally he got close enough to see into my sister's car.

His eyes bulged.

His jaw dropped.

His lower lip quivered.

"Lanny Shanks?" he gasped.

35

It took a while for Principal Blanco to get all the women to leave. Then he told Josh and Andy to go to class and Jessica to go over to the high school. That left him with me in Lanny's body.

"I think you better come to my office, Miss Shanks." He led me to the office and held the door for me. I ducked past him. Principal Blanco closed the office door.

"Please have a seat." Principal Blanco gestured to a chair. "Can I get you anything?"

Lanny's throat felt a little dry. "Some water?"

"Certainly." Principal Blanco left the office, then came back a moment later carrying a white Styrofoam cup.

"Here," he said.

"Oh, thank you."

Principal Blanco went around to his side of the desk and sat down. For a second he just stared at me while I sipped the water.

"Are you all right?" he asked.

"Yes, I think so." In Lanny's body I took an-other sip of the water and felt the cool liquid run down Lanny's long throat. Principal Blanco kept gazing at me with a dreamy look in his eyes. Something about it started to make me feel ner-vous.

"Lanny Shanks," he said.

"Well, not exactly."

A broad grin appeared on Principal Blanco's face. "Very funny. I didn't realize you had such a good sense of humor."

"I wasn't making a joke," I said in Lanny's body.

"Of course not." Principal Blanco smiled. "The one and only Lanny Shanks. Without a doubt the most beautiful woman in the world. The face on every magazine cover and in ads on a hundred different TV channels. Now sitting in my office pretending she's someone else. I understand com-pletely."

"You do?" I asked, surprised.

Principal Blanco leaned forward. "Fame isn't all it's cracked up to be, is it? There's no privacy. No personal life. No chance to sit back and just breathe and feel. No time to stop and smell the flowers. You're tired of it, aren't you?"

I nodded Lanny's head.

Principal Blanco leaned even closer. "Lanny, I realize this may sound a bit abrupt, but I can give you something no one else can. It may sound crazy, but please hear me out. Several years ago I visited an island in the South Pacific. It's near Bora-Bora and it's the closest place to heaven I've ever seen. I've got some money in the bank. Enough for two one-way tickets to paradise. What do you say, Lanny? Run away with me. Come, be my love, and we will discover the world anew."

"Aren't you married?" I asked in Lanny's body.

Principal Blanco's jaw fell open with surprise and he sat back in his chair. "How did you know . . . uh, I mean, I'm flattered that you cared enough to find out."

"And you've got some kids," I said in Lanny's body.

Once again Principal Blanco leaned forward. "Lanny, my darling, let me explain. Yes, I have children, but they're all out of the house and in college now. Yes, I am married, but — " He let out a long slow breath. "The flame of passion is long gone. My wife and I live like strangers sharing the same house. I hardly know who she is anymore."

Briiinnng! The phone on Principal Blanco's desk rang and he answered it. "Hello? Oh, er, hi, hon, I'm busy right now. Can I call you back? What? The dry cleaning? Sure, I'll pick it up on the way home, but . . . The dog got out again? How many times have I told you to keep the gate closed? Yes, but I can't talk right now about . . .

Our anniversary is tomorrow? Uh, of course I remembered. Yes, our favorite restaurant is fine, but . . . No! Your sister and her bratty kids *cannot* stay with us, and that's final!"

Principal Blanco hung up. His face looked red.

"You may not know who *she* is anymore," I said in Lanny's body, "but she sure seems to know who *you* are."

Principal Blanco got up and came around the desk. He got down on one knee and took Lanny's hand in his. "Lanny, er, Miss Shanks, please hear me out. I am mortal, only made of flesh and blood, but *you* are a goddess. I worship the very ground you walk on. I dream of you at night. Let me take you away from all this! I promise I will always treat you like a queen."

Principal Blanco started to pull Lanny's hand toward him as if he wanted to plant a big, wet kiss on her knuckles. We had entered the realm of gross. I knew it was time to get out. No matter what happened outside the office, it had to be better than being slobbered on by my principal.

In Lanny's body, I jumped out from the seat and yanked my hand away. I headed for the door, but Principal Blanco got there first. He pressed his back against the door and held out his hands to stop me.

"Miss Shanks, please stop!" he begged.

In Lanny's body I stopped.

"Don't go, please!" Principal Blanco said. "You

don't understand what this means to me. You can't! The nights I've dreamed of you! *Yearned* for you!" Principal Blanco fell to his knees in front of the door and clasped his hands. "Please, Miss Shanks, come away and be my love! I'll worship the very ground you walk on!"

Principal Blanco started to bend forward toward the floor. For a second I thought he was going to kiss Lanny's feet!

In Lanny's body I quickly stepped back. Principal Blanco kept leaning forward. A moment later he kissed the floor where I'd just stood.

There was no doubt about it. He may have been my principal, but he was also one sick puppy.

Then the office door opened.

And there stood Angus!

36

Angus stared down at Principal Blanco, who was still on his hands and knees with his butt sticking up in the air as he kissed the carpet. Then Angus looked at me in Lanny's body.

"Is this the guy?" Angus asked.

I didn't know what to say. Meanwhile, Principal Blanco looked up. His jaw dropped. He quickly got to his feet and dusted off his knees. "Who are you?"

"I'm Angus Bangus," said Angus. "What kind of a nut case are you?"

"I happen to be the principal of this school." Principal Blanco puffed out his chest. "Angus Bangus? What kind of name is that?"

"What kind of principal licks the carpet?" Angus asked back.

"I wasn't licking the carpet," Principal Blanco sputtered. "I was, er, uh, looking for something."

"What?" asked Angus.

"A contact lens," Principal Blanco said.

"Whose contact lens?" asked Angus.

"Uh, Miss Shanks's."

"Miss Shanks don't wear contacts, meat brain."

"What are you doing here?" asked Principal Blanco. "What do you want?"

Angus turned to me in Lanny's body. "I was wrong. I was thinking too much about me and not enough about us. If you want to renounce the Pledge of Veg, that's fine. If you want to consume sugar and caffeine, that's your business. The point is, I love you. Can you forgive me? Will you take me back?"

"Wait!" Principal Blanco suddenly gasped. "Lanny, don't listen to him! He's already admitted he thinks too much about himself. I, on the other hand, have always thought of you and only you! Cast your lot with me, Lanny!"

"Cast your lot?" Angus scowled. "What cave did you crawl out of?"

"It's poetry, you low-life head banger," Principal Blanco shot back. "The language of love."

Angus rolled his eyes and turned to me in Lanny's body. "You can't be serious about this fruitcake, Lanny. You step out of line and he'll give you detention."

"Don't listen to him!" Principal Blanco cried. "Think of what he does for a living. What kind of future can he give you? These bands are big for a week and then disappear forever. A year from now he'll be serving burgers at McDonald's."

"Oh, yeah?" Angus snapped. "I drive a Ferrari Superrossa. What do you drive? A Yugo?"

"A Camry LE, for your information," Principal Blanco replied with a huff. "What did you get on your SATs?"

"My what?" Angus scowled.

"Your Scholastic Achievement Tests," Principal Blanco said. "Your college boards. You *did* go to college, didn't you?"

"My last CD went quintuple platinum, you twerp in a suit," Angus shot back. "Last summer my band sold out every stadium from L.A. to Tokyo. I could buy everything you've got with the change in my pocket."

"Money isn't everything!" Principal Blanco shouted.

"Only losers say that!" Angus yelled.

"Oh, yeah?" yelled Principal Blanco. "You're so dumb you tried to read an audiobook."

"You're so poor you eat cereal with a fork to save milk," Angus shot back.

"You're so stupid you took a spoon to the Superbowl."

"You're so broke, when burglars break into your house they leave *you* money."

"You're so thick you watch *The Three Stooges* and take notes!"

They were so busy trading cut-downs that neither noticed when I slipped out the door and left the office.

110

I got out into the hall. Amazingly, it was empty. My first thought was to get out of school and then figure out what to do. But going out the main entrance wouldn't work. I'd have to go through the lobby and I was bound to be noticed. That left the gym or the exit at the end of the science wing.

The science wing was a lot closer, and I decided to head for it. I was lucky. In Lanny's body I managed to get there without being seen. I hurried down the hall toward the doors.

Suddenly a voice called out, "Stop!"

37

I spun around. Behind me was Mr. Dirksen.

"Can I help you?"

"How?" I asked in Lanny's body.

"You seem lost." Mr. Dirksen pointed back down the hall. "The classrooms are that way."

"I'm not looking for a classroom."

Mr. Dirksen frowned. "You're not a substitute?"

"Do I *look* like a substitute?"

Mr. Dirksen stepped closer and squinted at me in Lanny's body. He started at the top of Lanny's head and went down to her toes and back up again.

He rubbed his chin.

He scratched his head.

Then he said, "You're young and female, so I would say, yes, you *do* look like a substitute."

In Lanny's body I put my hand on my hip. "Have you ever seen a substitute who was *this* beautiful?"

Mr. Dirksen scowled. "Some are quite attractive."

"*This* attractive?" I arched one of Lanny's eyebrows.

"Don't you think you're being a bit conceited?" Mr. Dirksen asked.

This was getting ridiculous. "Mr. Dirksen, it's me, Jake Sherman."

Mr. Dirksen's eyebrows rose. "Jake?"

"Yours truly."

"Why would you switch bodies with a substitute?" Mr. Dirksen asked. Sometimes he could be incredibly thick.

"She's *not* a substitute!" I insisted. "She's the most beautiful woman in the world."

"But what does she do?" Mr. Dirksen asked.

"She doesn't have to *do* anything! All she has to do is be beautiful."

"And she gets paid for that?" Mr. Dirksen asked.

"Millions of dollars."

"Interesting," Mr. Dirksen said. "Well, I think you've finally switched with the right person, Jake. Good luck."

The next thing I knew, Mr. Dirksen turned and headed back toward his lab.

"Wait!" I cried.

Mr. Dirksen stopped. "What?"

"I don't want to be in this body!" I cried.

"What about the millions of dollars?" Mr. Dirksen asked.

I thought of having to choose between Angus Bangus and Principal Blanco. "It's not worth it."

"Hmmm." Mr. Dirksen rubbed his chin again. "Maybe I should switch with you."

"What about Ms. Rogers?"

"I'm sure she wouldn't mind all that money," Mr. Dirksen said.

"I think she'd mind that you turned into a girl."

"Oh, good point," Mr. Dirksen admitted. "So, I suppose you want to switch back into your own body?"

"The sooner the better."

"Go find your body and bring it to the science lab," Mr. Dirksen said.

"I can't," I said. "If I go anywhere in this body I'll be mobbed."

Mr. Dirksen let out another big sigh. "Okay. Wait in the lab. I'll go find you."

Mr. Dirksen left to go find Lanny in my body. In the meantime, I went into the science lab and started to pull the blue tarp off the big DITS. At the same time, I could feel Lanny's stomach begin to rumble hungrily again. It was amazing. It felt like she was *always* half starved. It might have been cool to be a supermodel, but I wasn't sure it was worth starving for.

I heard a click as the doorknob turned. *Great!* I thought. *Mr. Dirksen found Lanny in my body.* In a few minutes I would be back in my own body again.

The door swung open.

But it wasn't Lanny in my body and Mr. Dirksen.

It was Amanda Gluck!

And behind her came Barry Dunn with Josh!

38

"Let me go!" Josh squirmed and struggled to get away from Barry, who had one of Josh's arms twisted behind his back.

Barry hardly heard him. He was too busy staring at me in Lanny's body. "Whoa! What a babe!"

"I know that's . . . *Snork!* . . . you, Jake," Amanda said to me in Lanny's body. "Here's the deal. You . . . *Snork!* . . . switch bodies with me . . . *Snork!* . . . or Barry tortures Josh."

"Don't do it, Jake!" Josh cried.

"Why do you want to be in Lanny's body?" I asked. "I thought you were totally against all this stuff."

"I *was* against it as long as . . . *Snork!* . . . I thought I had to be in my body," Amanda explained. "It's totally unfair that people . . . *Snork!* . . . judge other people by their appearance. But I . . . *Snork!* . . . have to be practical, Jake. People aren't going to change. They're . . . *Snork!* . . . always going to be shallow and superficial. If that's

116

the way ... *Snork!* ... it's going to be, then I'd be out of my mind not to take advantage of this situation."

"Just let me warn you," I said in Lanny's body. "It's not so great to be in this body. You starve all the time. You never want to go out in the sun because it'll wreck your skin. And you have to wrap yourself in avocado mush every night."

"I can ... *Snork!* ... live with that," Amanda replied. "Let's switch bodies."

I stared at Barry holding Josh. I stared at the DITS. Then I stared back at Amanda, the worst brownnose do-gooder kiss-up in school, a girl only the World's Ugliest Cross-eyed Cow could love. Suddenly I had a horrible thought.

I might not have liked being in Lanny's body.

But being in Amanda's body was going to be a whole lot worse!

39

"Are you going to . . . *Snork!* . . . switch with me or not?" Amanda demanded.

"Don't do it, Jake!" Josh gasped. "You can't let Amanda into Lanny's body! And you can't let yourself go into Amanda's body! It's a fate worse than death! I don't care what Barry does to me! Don't do it!"

"What should I do?" Barry asked Amanda.

"It's Monkey Bite time," Amanda replied coldly.

Barry curled his hand into a claw.

"I changed my mind!" Josh suddenly cried. "Go ahead, Jake, switch with Amanda. Be my guest! I think it's a great idea!"

"I thought you were going to be brave," I said.

"I was," Josh said. "But being brave can hurt and I hate pain."

Amanda smiled triumphantly and nodded toward the DITS. "Let's . . . *Snork!* . . . go, Jake."

"Barry, what did Amanda promise to get you to do this?" I asked in Lanny's body.

"She said I'd be her boyfriend, and she'd help me be a famous male model," Barry answered.

"The only thing you could model are straitjackets," Josh muttered.

Barry lowered the Monkey Bite onto Josh's shoulder.

"Ow!" Josh screamed in pain. "I was only kidding, Barry. You'll make a great male model, really."

"Just remember, Barry," I said in Lanny's body. "You might be Lanny Shanks's boyfriend, but it'll really be Amanda inside Lanny Shanks's body."

Barry just shrugged.

Amanda crossed her arms. "I'm . . . *Snork!* . . . getting tired of all . . . *Snork!* . . . this talk. Now are you going to . . . *Snork!* . . . give me Lanny's body or do I make Barry . . . *Snork!* . . . put the Double Monkey Bite on Josh?"

The Double Monkey Bite was one claw on that muscle between the neck and shoulder and the other on the muscle just above the knee. It was the sheer ultimate in painful torture.

"Switch, Jake," Josh whimpered. "I promise I'll be nice to you, even if you're in Amanda's body. Even if you snort forever. *Please!*"

I hated to do it. I hated the idea of being in Amanda Gluck's body. I hated the idea of wearing her thick glasses and going around snorting nervously. Even worse was the thought of Amanda in Lanny's body. But for Josh's sake, I said yes.

40

*W*HUMP!
      I opened Amanda Gluck's eyes. I knew I
was in her body. The room was a blur. A fuzzy
shape moved toward me and held out a pair of
thick glasses. I put them on. The fuzzy shape
turned into Josh.

"I just want to say thank you, Jake," he said
solemnly. "You've made the ultimate sacrifice.
You're a true friend."

I knew what he meant. I had just gone from being the world's most beautiful woman to . . . well,
being Amanda Gluck.

The lab door swung open. Principal Blanco and
Angus Bangus rushed in.

"What's going on in here?" Principal Blanco demanded. Then he blinked. "Why am I even asking? Okay, who's who *this* time?"

I raised Amanda's hand. "I'm Jake."

Barry raised his hand. "I'm Barry."

Josh raised his hand. "I'm Britney Spears."

Principal Blanco scowled for a moment, then turned to Amanda in Lanny's body. "Amanda?"

"Not anymore," answered Amanda in Lanny's body.

Angus Bangus stepped up to Amanda in Lanny's body. "Listen, I don't care who you are. I love you and I want you to come back to me."

A big smile appeared on Amanda in Lanny's face. "Can I go for a ride in your car?"

"Lanny, or whoever you are," said Angus. "You can *have* my car."

"Wait!" Barry yelped. "Amanda, you promised you'd be *my* girlfriend now."

"Oh, give me a break." Amanda rolled Lanny's eyes.

"What about me?" cried Principal Blanco.

"All of you, get a grip," said Amanda in Lanny's body. "Angus is a rich and famous rock star and now I'm a rich and famous supermodel. The rest of you are nobodies. Just go back to your pathetic little lives. Angus and I are going back to the big time."

And with that, Amanda in Lanny's body slid her arm through Angus's and they swept out of the science lab.

41

The lab grew quiet. You never saw a more miserable bunch of guys. At least Barry, Principal Blanco, and I in Amanda's body were miserable.

"Hey, guys, come on," said Josh. "It's not that bad."

"What are you talking about?" Barry sputtered. "I just lost the chance to be a world-famous male model."

"And I just lost the girl of my dreams," wailed Principal Blanco.

"I don't know what you guys are so upset about," I said in Amanda's body. "At least you don't have to spend the rest of your life in *this* body."

Principal Blanco and Barry traded a look. "Guess we don't have it so bad, huh?" Barry said.

Principal Blanco nodded.

The lab door swung open. Mr. Dirksen and Lanny in my body came in.

"Where is she?" Mr. Dirksen asked.

"She just left for the big time," Principal Blanco answered.

Mr. Dirksen's mouth fell open. "Jake left in that woman's body?"

"No," I said in Amanda's body. "Amanda Gluck left in that woman's body."

Mr. Dirksen blinked with astonishment. "Jake? Now you're in Amanda's body?"

I nodded.

"I'm sorry to hear that," Mr. Dirksen said.

"Me, too," I said in Amanda's body. Suddenly I realized something and turned to Lanny in my body. "Unless you'll let me have my body back."

Lanny in my body straightened up nervously.

"Come on, Lanny," I said in Amanda's body. "Didn't you say you didn't really care whose body you were in?"

"I . . . I did," Lanny in my body admitted. "But . . . there's a limit."

"Let me guess," I groaned in Amanda's body. "The limit stops just short of being Amanda Gluck?"

Lanny nodded my head. "Sorry, Jake, you're a nice kid, and I'd like to help you, but if that was the last body on Earth I think I'd rather switch with my dog."

"Funny you should mention that," Josh muttered.

"Josh," I said in Amanda Gluck's body. "You're

one of my two best friends in the whole world. You'll still be my friend even if I'm in this body, right?"

"Uh . . ." Josh hesitated. "Maybe three days a year."

"I know!" Principal Blanco said. "One would be Halloween."

"Right," said Josh.

"And April Fools' Day?" said Barry.

Josh nodded. "Good guess."

"What's the third day?" asked Mr. Dirksen.

"Thanksgiving Day," said Josh.

"Why Thanksgiving?" asked Principal Blanco.

"Because we always go away," said Josh.

I bowed Amanda's head in despair. It was hopeless. Lanny wouldn't give me my body back. Amanda Gluck would spend the rest of her life as the most beautiful woman in the world (could you blame her?). And I was doomed.

And that's when the lab door opened and Angus Bangus rushed back in.

42

Angus looked pale and scared. His right eye was twitching. "I need help!"

"Why?" asked Lanny in my body. "Where's Amanda?"

"Who?" asked Angus.

"The person who's now in Lanny's body," I said.

"She's in the Ferrari," Angus said. "She won't get out."

"Why not?" I asked in Amanda's body.

"Because she doesn't want to," said Angus. "But I can't take it. Someone has to get her out of the car."

"Why?" asked Mr. Dirksen.

"Because she snorts!" Angus said. "And all she wants to talk about is Barbie. If I have to spend another minute with her I'll go insane! I don't care whose body she's in!"

43

It took all day to get Amanda in Lanny's body out of the Ferrari. It wasn't like we could call the police and tell them what had happened, so we just waited until she really needed to use the bathroom.

In the end we all switched back into our own bodies. Amanda went back to her campaign against unrealistic body images. Principal Blanco was kind of brokenhearted, but Lanny wrote on her poster about how nice it was to meet him and how they'd always be friends. When you go into the office now, the poster's in a frame hanging on the wall.

A couple of months later Amber, Andy, Josh, and I were sitting in my kitchen working on our saliva bubbles again. My friends and I watched in awe as Amber managed to launch not one but *two* bubbles at once.

"A double!" Josh announced.

"It's unheard of!" cried Andy.

Amber beamed proudly. We heard a door bang and Jessica came in with the mail. "This is for you, Jake." She handed me a thick, square letter. My name and address were written in fancy lettering.

"Looks like an invitation," said Josh.

"A wedding invitation," said Amber.

I tore open the envelope. The inside was lined with thin gold paper and there were some cards and an envelope separated with thin pink tissue.

"Wow, fancy," said Andy.

"Who's it from?" asked Jessica.

I pulled out a card written in the same fancy lettering as the address:

Mr. and Mrs. Leonard Bumkiss
invite you to the wedding of
their son, Allen Bumkiss, to
Miss Louise Snerd . . .

"Who are Allen Bumkiss and Louise Snerd?" Jessica asked.

"I don't have a . . ." I began to say, then stopped. "Oh, my gosh! Allen Bumkiss, Angus Bangus. Louise Snerd, Lanny Shanks."

"You think?" Amber asked.

"Look." Josh pointed at the invitation. "The wedding's in California and everyone's asked to bring their favorite vegetable."

"It must be them!" Jessica gasped. "But why use their real names?"

"Famous people do that all the time," Amber said. "To avoid publicity when they want something to be private."

"Are you going to go, Jake?" Josh asked.

"All the way to California?" I said. "It's doubtful."

"Could I go instead?" Jessica asked.

"No."

"If you're not going, can we have the invitation?" asked Andy.

"No."

"We could sell the information about the wedding to a gossip columnist," said Josh.

"No."

"Can't we at least tell everyone at school that you were invited to the wedding?" asked Andy.

"No."

"Why not?" asked Josh.

"Because it's dumb and phony and it just doesn't matter," I said.

Andy's shoulders sagged with disappointment. "Oh, great. So we just go back to our little, unimportant lives here in the middle of nowhere?"

"I don't think our lives are unimportant," said Amber. "They're as important as anyone else's."

"We're not famous," said Andy.

"We can blow double saliva bubbles," countered Amber.

"We're not rich," said Josh.

"We can go out in the sun and not worry," I said.

"We don't have a Ferrari," said Jessica.

"We don't *need* a Ferrari," I said.

"Okay, okay," Josh mumbled. "We get the point. Life in Jeffersonville is beautiful. Everything's wonderful and it's great to be alive."

I winked at Amber. "Exactly."

About the Author

Todd Strasser has written many award-winning novels for young and teenage readers. Among his best-known books are *Help! I'm Trapped in Obedience School* and *Help! I'm Trapped in Santa's Body*. His most recent books for Scholastic are *Help! I'm Trapped in a Professional Wrestler's Body* and *Help! I'm Trapped in a Vampire's Body*.

The movie *Next to You*, starring Melissa Joan Hart, was based on Todd's novel *How I Created My Perfect Prom Date*.

Todd speaks frequently at schools about the craft of writing and conducts writing workshops for young people. He and his family live outside New York City with their yellow Labrador retriever, Mac.

You can find out more about Todd and his books at http://www.toddstrasser.com